It wasn't the worst thing in the world . . .

But it was awful! I wouldn't be with my friends — my team. I wanted to take a huge eraser and wipe the whole thing out — make everything go back to the way it had been before.

I knew that having to quit gymnastics didn't rank up there with life's great tragedies. Yet it felt like such a big deal to me. And I felt so sad. I wouldn't be a Pinecone anymore — I wasn't going to be at the gym, and that's where we all belonged — together at the gym.

**Look for these and other books
in THE GYMNASTS series:**

THE GYMNASTS

#20 THE GYMNASTS' GIFT

Elizabeth Levy

AN
APPLE
PAPERBACK

SCHOLASTIC INC.
New York Toronto London Auckland Sydney

ISBN 0-590-44693-2

12 11 10 9 8 7 6 5 4 3 2   1 2 3 4 5 6/9

Printed in the U.S.A.   28

First Scholastic printing, November 1991

To Ona and Isa
who always wanted a Christmas book

Santa Doesn't Like It When You're Greedy

I should have known something bad was going to happen. Things started to go wrong the day my dog, Cleo, ate one of my favorite gymnastics shoes.

My best friend, Lauren Baca, thought it was a riot when I pulled the gnawed piece of leather out of my knapsack, in the locker room at the Evergreen Gymnastics Academy.

"It's Cindi's ruined slipper. Get it? Like Cinderella?" shouted Lauren to the other kids in the room.

I heard a high-pitched little giggle across the locker room. Our coach, Patrick Harmon, had recently started a Tiny Tots Gymnastics program for kids under five.

1

I waved my chewed slipper in the air. The little kids giggled some more. I like little kids. Maybe it's because I'm the youngest in my family. I've got four older brothers, and I always wanted to be someone's big sister.

"Cindi-ella, Cindi-ella," sang Lauren. When we were in kindergarten together, Lauren used to call me Cindi-ella. I hated that name.

"You haven't called me that in years," I said.

Lauren grinned. "Do you still hate it?"

"Hate what?" asked my teammate Jodi Sutton. Our team is called the Pinecones. We're tight. We've been together for a couple of years now, and we know each other really well.

Jodi loves jokes, but I didn't want her teasing me, too.

"Don't tell her — " I started to beg Lauren.

"Cindi-ella!" she blurted out before I could finish my sentence. "Cindi-ella's slipper's ruined."

"Oh, shut up," I said.

Lauren looked guilty. "You're not really mad at me, are you?" she asked.

I shook my head. It was hard to stay mad at Lauren, especially for using a nickname from kindergarten. "No," I admitted.

"Good," said Lauren. "No use crying over a chewed slipper."

"Yeah, but do you know what these things cost?" I groaned. "I'm way over my allowance anyhow." My parents pay for my lessons, but I'm supposed to pay for my gymnastics clothes out of my clothing budget.

"So?" Jodi shrugged. "Put it on your Christmas list."

"Yeah," I muttered, "like I really want to get gymnastics shoes for Christmas. That's real exciting."

"What *do* you want?" Lauren asked.

I didn't answer. I wanted a new mountain bike with twenty-one gears, instead of my old clunker three-speed, but I thought it was too expensive.

"I'm hoping for black velvet leggings," said Ti An Thruong, who's only nine.

"Oh me, too," gushed Darlene.

I had to laugh. "Darlene, how many pairs of velvet leggings do you already have?" I asked her.

Darlene held her hand up and started to count on her fingers. "I've got the red pair and the black pair and, oh, yeah, one royal-blue, but I saw a pair of green crushed velvet — they were so hot."

I should explain about Darlene. She sounds spoiled, but she's actually one of the nicest kids I know. Her dad is "Big Beef" Broderick, a star football player for the Denver Broncos, and I guess Darlene can buy pretty much whatever she wants. Darlene loves clothes. I hate to shop, which is lucky because I don't have much money to spend.

"I want a new skateboard," said Jodi.

I kept quiet. Listening to my friends made me a little uncomfortable. Nobody's rich, except maybe Darlene, but everybody seemed so sure they could get whatever they wanted.

My dad is a commercial pilot with Trans American Airlines, the big airline. People think he's got lots of money, but pilots don't make *that* much, and my mom stays at home and helps us kids. Dad always says that raising five kids is a full-time job. Christopher and Stephen are in college. Tim's a junior in high school this year, and he's a real brain. He's probably going to apply to Ivy League colleges in the East. Jared and I are the two babies of the family. Jared's thirteen, and I'm eleven. Jared and I both take gymnastics, but Jared goes only twice a week, and I go four times.

I know money's tight in our house. I shouldn't have even hoped for a mountain bike.

I shoved the ruined shoe deeper into my knapsack. Maybe I would put gymnastics shoes on my Christmas wish list after all.

"I want velvet leggings for Hanukkah," said Ashley.

"That's on my list, too," said Jodi. "I want velvet leggings, and I want a new jacket, maybe one with leather sleeves." Jodi surprised me. She's usually no more into clothes than I am.

"Watch it, Jodi," teased Lauren. "Santa doesn't like it when you're too greedy."

Jodi looked a little guilty.

"I can't believe that you Pinecones are still talking about Santa Claus," said Becky Dyson. "Only babies believe in Santa." Becky is thirteen. She's on the advanced team, the Needles, and she practically makes a career out of hating the Pinecones.

"Shh, Becky," I warned her. I cocked my chin toward the little kids. I didn't want Becky ruining Christmas for them. Besides, I still half believed in Santa Claus myself.

Becky looked disgusted. "You all sound like a bunch of spoiled rich kids," she said.

We stared at her. Becky goes to private school, and if there was anybody whom I'd call a spoiled rich kid, it would be her.

"Oh, yeah?" said Jodi. "What do you want for Christmas? A Rolls-Royce?"

"I'm asking everyone I know to give the money they'd spend on gifts to the Save the Evergreens Fund," said Becky.

"Really?" asked Darlene.

Becky nodded. "I think we all have too much stuff already," she said.

We got very quiet and looked at each other.

Becky left the locker room, holding her head up high as if she were adjusting her halo.

"Well, that's a downer," said Jodi. "I think she just said that to annoy us. I don't believe her."

Darlene looked thoughtful. "Becky has a point," she said. "Maybe we *are* too caught up in material things."

"Personally, if Becky's into saving evergreens, I want to be a lumberjack," said Jodi.

We laughed, but a little bit uneasily.

Then we went out into the gym.

Stick It to the Pinecones

The beam is the great equalizer. All the money in the world can't help you land straight on a four-inch board, four feet above the ground. I did a back flip and a back walkover and landed them both with a solid thunk.

Patrick, our coach, was standing by the beam, grinning up at me. "Way to go, Cindi," he said. "I might schedule you for beam in the Holiday Show." Every year we put on an exhibition in December. It's fun because it's not competitive, like a meet. It's just a chance to show off to our parents and friends.

"I thought I'd do bars," I said. Bars are my best event. I looked over at the bars where Heidi Ferguson was working out with Dimitri Vickorskoff.

7

Heidi is so good. She is way beyond Becky's group, the Needles. She's a world-class athlete who just happens to love our gym.

Patrick smiled up at me. "Actually, Cindi, what I like about you is that I could put you anywhere and you'd shine."

I lapped up the compliment. Patrick doesn't give praise that freely, and his words made me incredibly happy.

I hopped down from the beam to give Jodi a chance. She was a little unsteady on her mount, but then she calmed down. Jodi used to be the most wobbly of all of us on the beam, but she's gotten much better.

Lauren was chewing her thumb, looking anxious.

"What's the problem?" I asked her. "This is just practice."

"I'm wondering about the Holiday Show," said Lauren.

"Don't worry," I said, still basking in Patrick's praise. "The Holiday Show is just a goof — Patrick'll probably have you demonstrate vault — that's your best event."

"That wasn't what I was talking about," said Lauren, sounding really annoyed.

I stared at her. "What's gotten into you?" I asked her. "I didn't call you Baca-laca." That used to be *my* nickname for Lauren, and she hated it as much as I hated "Cindi-ella."

"What Becky said really got to me," said Lauren. "Didn't it bother you?"

I shrugged. "Becky always bothers me, but so what?" I said.

"Yeah, but this time she might be right. Maybe we all are a little spoiled. Should I tell my parents and aunts and uncles that I don't want any presents?"

I snorted. "That'll be the day," I said.

"I'm serious," said Lauren. "I think maybe we should all give up our presents to save the evergreens this year."

There was a weird silence in the gym. It was just one of those moments when suddenly there's a pocket of silence, and Lauren's words rang from the rafters.

"What's that, Lauren?" asked Patrick. Jodi had finished her beam routine, and Patrick was standing by the beam.

"I was thinking," said Lauren, a little louder now that she realized everybody in the gym was listening to her. "Maybe we should dedicate the Holiday Show to the Save the Evergreens Fund."

"Hey!" shouted Becky from across the room where the Needles were working on their vaults. "That was *my* idea!"

"I know," said Lauren. "I wasn't trying to steal it."

"Lauren, that's not a bad idea," said Patrick.

"My idea!" said Becky, barreling across the room. She put her hands on her hips and glared at us. "Patrick, the Pinecones are trying to steal my suggestion."

"We're not stealing anything. It wasn't your idea to do our Holiday Show as a benefit," I argued. "It'll be perfect, because we're the Evergreen Gymnastics Academy, right, Patrick?"

Patrick nodded. "Let me look into it," he said.

"We could get our parents to donate prizes and have an auction like we do at my school," said Darlene. "I bet we could raise a lot of money."

"Hey, that's a great idea!" I said.

"I still say *I* should get credit," said Becky.

"You're right, Becky," said Darlene. "You made us think. It was your suggestion that got us started."

"Patrick, it's not fair," said Becky, racing on as if Darlene hadn't said anything.

Patrick was looking mighty confused. "I don't understand, Becky. The Pinecones are saying that it *was* you who made them think about doing this. What's your problem?"

Becky stammered. "Well . . . uh . . . I *was* going to talk to you about doing the Holiday Show as a benefit."

"You didn't mention that in the locker room," said Ti An. "You just said something about giving up all your Christmas presents."

"You Pinecones can't take the credit for it," said Becky, sounding like a broken record.

"Becky, we are giving you credit," I said. It was pretty funny. For once Becky did have a good idea, and when we tried to tell her, all she could do was get mad at the Pinecones.

Becky stalked off.

"She is one piece of work," said Darlene.

"Why do you think she's so mad?" I asked Darlene.

She laughed. "I bet you anything in the world, Becky really doesn't care about the evergreens. She was just looking for a way to stick it to the Pinecones, and now we're sticking it to her."

3

That's Really Disgusting

I was surprised to see that my dad was home when I got back from gymnastics. Dad's schedule is always changing, but I knew that he was supposed to be flying to Seattle. He was sitting in the kitchen with the television on.

"Hi, Dad!" I said, giving him a kiss on his forehead. Lately there's been a lot more forehead to kiss. I get my thick, curly red hair from Dad. Dad's hair is just as thick as always in the back, but he's beginning to lose his hair in front.

"What's the problem?" I asked. "Is the airport closed 'cause of snow? It doesn't look that bad." Naturally we get a lot of bad weather in Denver in the winter, but Dad can usually fly unless the storm is really bad.

"The flight got canceled," said Dad, "but not because of weather."

"Where's Mom?" I asked.

"She's taking a bath," he said.

"I hope there's enough hot water," I said. Lately our water heater's been on the blink, and it's been driving Mom crazy. She always says it goes off right in the middle of her bath.

I opened the refrigerator and stared inside, not quite sure what I wanted. I couldn't decide between a yogurt and some leftover meat loaf.

"Cindi," said Dad. "How about closing the refrigerator door?" Mom has posted a sign on our refrigerator that reads, THIS IS NOT A LIBRARY. NO BROWSING, but I always forget.

"I can't decide. Do you want anything?"

Dad shook his head. I still had the door open. "Do you know how much electricity you're wasting?" he asked me. "You're the one who's always talking about protecting the environment by not wasting energy."

"I know, I know — it's not a library," I said. I got out the yogurt, an apple, and the meat loaf and peanut butter. "Dad, wait till you hear what we're going to do at the gym to save the evergreens."

Dad looked at the mixture. "Meat loaf and peanut butter?" he asked. "Mom and I made chili for tonight. Can't you wait for dinner?"

My parents make the best chili in the whole world.

"I'm starved," I said.

Dad gave me a half-smile. "Tell me about how the Pinecones plan to save the evergreens. I like the sound of that."

"It was great. We're getting ready for the Holiday Show, and we got the idea — well, actually it was sort of Becky's idea — to make it a benefit for the Save the Evergreens Fund."

"Becky?" asked Dad. He knows how I feel about Becky.

I nodded with my mouth full. "Sometimes even she has a good idea."

Just then the back door opened, and Jared charged in, followed by Cleo.

"There you are!" I shouted. "Boy, are you in trouble!"

"Me!" said Jared. "What did I do?"

"Not you. Cleo," I said.

Jared opened the refrigerator door and started browsing. "Hey," he said, "we're out of peanut butter."

"Don't you have eyes?" asked Dad, sounding annoyed. "Your sister has it right on the table. Close the refrigerator."

Jared didn't do it right away. He continued rummaging around until he found the mayonnaise. Then he got himself some dark pumpernickel bread and made himself a peanut-butter-and-mayonnaise sandwich.

Dad looked disgusted. "What kind of sandwich is that?"

"The mayonnaise makes the peanut butter slide down easily," said Jared with a grin. "I just discovered it."

"Has anybody around here ever heard of waiting until dinner?"

Jared and I both shook our heads.

"So, how were the old Pinecones today?" asked Jared. "You getting ready for the Holiday Show, too?"

"Yeah," I mumbled because my mouth was full of meat loaf and peanut butter. "That reminds me. Cleopatra!"

Cleo was sitting right under my feet, hoping for a few crumbs of meat loaf. She doesn't like peanut butter. It sticks to the roof of her mouth.

She was looking at me with her head cocked. She was giving me her "Aren't I adorable?" look. Cleo's a mutt, a red-and-brown terrier mix with cute little perky ears that fold down. People are always saying she looks just like the movie dog, Benji. To me, she looked like a dog in trouble.

"You!" I exploded at her. I got my knapsack. When I pulled out the chewed slipper, Cleo's stomach sank down against the floor, and she slowly backed away from me. When she was half-way under the table, she tried to skitter out the little doggy door we have in the back door.

"No, you don't," I said. I knew the only way to teach Cleo a lesson was to make sure that she knew she had done wrong. I grabbed her collar and waved the slipper at her nose.

"No! Bad girl!" I said.

Cleo's tail fell between her legs.

"What's this about?" Dad asked.

"Look at this," I said to Dad, tossing him the slipper. "It's ruined. She chewed it this morning. I'm going to need a new pair."

"She got one of my hockey gloves the other day," said Jared, talking with his mouth full.

Dad stared at the teeth marks on my slipper. "I can't believe the two of you!" he said.

Jared and I looked at each other. "What did we do wrong?" we asked in unison.

"You . . . are . . . you are . . . so careless," Dad said. "Why do you leave your things lying on the floor where Cleo can get them?"

Jared and I stopped eating. Despite his red hair and the cliché that redheads have bad tempers, Dad almost never raises his voice. He's one of the calmest people I know. But he sounded mad.

"Uh, Dad," said Jared, "I didn't chew it. Cleo did."

"She's just a dumb animal," said Dad. "You're supposed to have more brains. I hope you have

16

money in your allowance to pay for it. Hockey gloves are expensive."

"Dad, give me a break, it's Christmastime. I've got nothing left in my allowance."

"Neither do I," I said, looking down at my poor mutilated slipper. "And I'll need new shoes for the Holiday Show."

"And what's *your* excuse?" Dad asked me. "Why were you so thoughtless as to leave this around on the floor where Cleo couldn't help but be tempted?"

"Dad," I said, "I think you're forgetting something."

"What's that?" he asked.

"It's a slipper, Dad," I said. "It's a shoe. It belongs on the floor."

Dad looked a little embarrassed. He gave me a funny look and tossed the slipper on the floor. Cleo pounced on it, happily.

"Sorry," Dad mumbled. He pushed open the swinging door between our kitchen and dining room.

"What's gotten into him?" I asked Jared. "He got awfully upset about a chewed slipper and glove."

Jared just shrugged and took another bite of his peanut-butter-and-mayonnaise sandwich.

"That is really disgusting, you know," I said.

"I know," said Jared. "That's why I like it."

17

Can't Do Gymnastics and Worry

On Monday, Dad drove Jared and me to gymnastics. "Don't you have a flight scheduled?" I asked him.

"No," said Dad.

"How about for the rest of the week?" Jared asked.

"No," he said. Dad's never a chatterbox, but he seemed a little more quiet than usual.

"Well, I sure hope you don't have to work on the day of the Holiday Show," I said to him. "It's on December twenty-first."

"I think I'll be free," said Dad.

"Yeah, you wouldn't want to miss the Pinecones making fools of themselves," said Jared.

"What about you making a fool of yourself?" I

said. "You'll probably get stuck on the pommel horse — old peanut-butter breath."

"At least I don't put peanut butter on meat loaf," said Jared. "That's truly disgusting."

"Jared, Cindi, can't you do anything except fight?" asked Dad. Jared and I snickered. For us, this wasn't even fighting, it was just fooling around.

We pulled into the road behind the shopping mall. The mall was already lit up with Christmas decorations. All the trees were decorated with thousands of tiny white light bulbs. There was a giant Christmas tree in the middle of the parking lot and a menorah for Hanukkah.

"I can't wait till Christmas this year," said Jared. "I'm so psyched — Ryan knows what he's getting. His parents are giving him brand-new Rossignal skis — get it, Dad? Hint, hint."

"Doesn't Christmas mean anything to you except presents?" Dad asked.

"Uh, sure," said Jared. "But presents are nice, too."

"The Pinecones aren't just interested in gifts," I said proudly. "Remember, we got Patrick to make our Holiday Show a benefit for the Save the Evergreens Fund."

"I heard that was Becky's idea and you stole it," said Jared.

"That's not true!" I said.

"Will you kids stop fighting?" said Dad. "It's hard enough to drive in the snow." The snow was coming down pretty hard now, and although the street was plowed, snow was piled high along the sides of the road from the last snowstorm.

Jared jabbed me in the side with his elbow.

"Ouch!" I said, exaggerating a little. I punched him in the arm.

"Cut it out!" yelled Dad.

"He started it!" I said.

"She started it!" Jared said.

"I can't drive when you fight," said Dad. He stopped the car.

I looked out the window through the snow. I could see that Dad had pulled up as close to the gym as he could get through the snow. Jared was busy trying to punch me. "We're here, dodo," I said to him.

I opened the car door. Jared tripped me as I was getting out. I grabbed a pile of snow and tried to shove it down Jared's parka. He made a snowball and whizzed it by my head. I ducked, and it hit the windshield of a car coming toward us.

The car stopped. I realized it was Darlene and Big Beef.

"Jared did it, Big Beef!" I yelled, giggling. I knew that Jared absolutely idolized Darlene's dad.

Big Beef waved to my father, who got out of the car. "Hi, Mike," said Big Beef. "Maybe your son should be going to baseball practice, not gymnastics. He almost shattered my windshield."

Darlene grabbed her gym bag and climbed out of the car to walk up with us. Big Beef went over to the driver's side of our car to talk with Dad, and I realized I had left my gym bag in the backseat.

I scrambled back toward the car. I could hear Big Beef asking my dad, "Are the layoffs at TAA affecting you?"

Dad didn't answer. He waved his hand in the air as if warning Big Beef that he didn't want me to hear.

"I forgot my gym bag," I said quickly. "Sorry Jared and I got you so mad, Dad."

"Those two do nothing but fight," said Dad. "And I thought the older ones were bad."

"Hey, Dad!" shouted Darlene. "Maybe Mr. Jockett can get his airline to donate a free trip for our auction!"

Big Beef shook his head. "These kids," he said softly to my dad.

"Are you working on the auction, Big Beef?" asked Jared, sounding excited.

"Well, Darlene talked me into it," said Big Beef. "It's no big deal."

"That's super," I said. "Dad, do you think you can get the airline to donate a free trip? That would really get Becky's attention."

"Cindi," said Big Beef, a little sharply, "the point of this auction is not for the Pinecones to show up Becky."

I blushed. I didn't want Big Beef to think badly of me.

"Yeah, Dad," said Darlene, "but showing up Becky doesn't hurt."

I gave Darlene a grateful look.

"Get going, you kids," said Big Beef. "You're all going to be late."

I looked back at Dad. He seemed kind of sad, and his conversation with Big Beef had been strange. We trudged our way through the snow to the front door of the gym.

Jared put the hood of his parka over his head. He didn't try to throw any more snowballs. He always behaved himself around Darlene.

"That's so neat that your dad's working to save the evergreens," he said. "I'll bet our dad will be able to get the airline to donate a big prize."

"I wouldn't count on it," I said. I thought about the way Dad had sounded talking to Big Beef. We walked silently for a few minutes. I felt kind of funny. Dad had been acting a little weird.

"Jared, didn't you think Dad was in a bad mood?" I asked.

"He always hates it when we fight," said Jared.

We got close to door of the gym. The Evergreen Gymnastics Academy sounds pretty fancy, but it's just a gray concrete former warehouse. It's my favorite place in the whole world, though. I stopped worrying — you can't do gymnastics and worry.

5

Never Boring

When we shook the snow off our parkas, the warmth of the gym hit us like a blast furnace.

Patrick and Dimitri were watching Heidi on the trampoline. She was in a harness doing a double somersault. Heidi's family had donated the harness and trampoline to the gym when she had first started working out with us.

Jared, Darlene, and I stood and watched Heidi, too. She overrotated once and ended up doing a triple somersault.

She pointed her toes and gradually let the harness take her weight so she could stop.

She bounced up and down on the trampoline a couple of times and waved to us.

"Did you see that?" she exclaimed. "A triple!

Hey, Dimitri, think I can try that on my dismount from the high bar? Now *that's* an Olympic move!"

Dimitri shook his head. "Von mistake and already she vants to put it in the Olympics." But it was obvious that Dimitri was as excited as Heidi.

"Let me try it again," said Heidi.

Darlene shook her head. "Unbelievable!" We edged closer to the trampoline.

"What's she trying to do?" asked Jared. "I don't get it."

"A triple somersault," I said. "With Heidi, anything's possible."

Becky was watching Heidi, too. "Dimitri and Heidi have both gone off their rockers," she said. "No girl's ever done a triple-somersault dismount from the high bar."

"Heidi can be the first," I said. It was what I loved about gymnastics, the feeling that anything was possible.

We changed quickly in the locker room and came back out into the gym. Heidi had finished with the trampoline.

She was toweling herself off as we were doing our warm-ups.

"Do you really think you can do a triple somersault for real from the high bar?" I asked her. "Has it ever been done before?"

Heidi grinned. There was *nothing* she liked more then trying something that had never been done before. "Well, I sure can't do it without the harness yet," she said. "That was my very first time."

"It's a proven fact that *nobody*'s ever done a triple somersault as a dismount," said Lauren.

"Well, that's the challenge," said Heidi. "It'll take me a couple of months, but I'll bet I can do it."

"Someday I'd like to try just a plain old double," I said.

"You can do it," said Heidi. "You've got a lot of power in your turning."

"I do?" I asked. I couldn't believe Heidi thought I was that good.

"Sure," said Heidi. "Ask Patrick. Maybe he'll let you work in the harness today. I don't need it anymore."

"Patrick!" I yelled. "Can I try to do what Heidi was doing?"

"Oh, give me a break," said Becky. "Talk about delusions of grandeur . . ."

"I didn't mean a triple somersault," I said. "I just want to see what I can do."

"Why not?" said Patrick. "I'll want somebody besides Heidi to demonstrate trampoline for the Holiday Show. Maybe we'll work something out. I can put Jodi on the beam."

"That'll be a shocker for my mom," said Jodi. Jodi's mom is a world-class gymnast herself, and her specialty was the beam. It's always been Jodi's worst event.

"I think I'll stick to the tramp," said Jodi. She grabbed the edge of the trampoline and somersaulted onto it. She stood up and did some warm-up jumps, going higher and higher. Patrick watched her.

"Okay, I'll try the triple!" shouted Jodi.

"Jodi!" snapped Patrick. "Off of there! Nobody's trying anything without the harness. You can warm up on the trampoline, but nobody tries anything new without the harness."

Jodi looked annoyed. Safety's never been a number-one issue with Jodi.

"Off!" commanded Patrick. "I said Cindi could try it. I want you over on the low beam."

I went to the side of the trampoline and put the harness around my waist. It has an adjustable ring, so that it holds you up but at the same time allows you to twist freely.

Patrick asked me to put on the light helmet. "Are you worried I'll crack my head?" I asked him.

"Trying anything new on the tramp can be dangerous," he said. I put on the leather helmet and began to bounce up and down, letting my momentum carry me higher and higher.

"Okay," said Patrick, "next bounce, try a single."

I felt as if I were a giant about twelve feet tall. From the height of my jump, I could see the whole gym spread out below me. It's such an incredible feeling of freedom.

I pointed my toes, and when I hit the trampoline I bent my knees so that I'd get more power. This time I went higher and higher. Just before my body was beginning to be dragged back down to earth, I twisted my head down toward the floor. For some reason, I forgot to tuck my knees under me. I ended up doing a complete turn in the air with my body straight as a board. Luckily my feet ended up underneath me, and I bounced back down to the trampoline. I let myself bounce a few times until I could stop.

"Sorry, Patrick," I said.

Patrick was laughing. So was Dimitri. Heidi was looking at me with her mouth open.

"What?" I asked a little nervously.

"It was a perfect layout twist," said Patrick. "If I had asked you to do it, you'd never have made it."

"It's much harder than a regular somersault," said Heidi.

"It is?" I exclaimed. "It was a goofy mistake. I just forgot to bend my knees."

"It's our Christmas gift," said Dimitri. "Von

girl does a triple by mistake, another does a lay-out by mistake — vith mistakes like this ve can go straight to the Olympics!"

I bounced up and down some more.

"Come on, Patrick," I said. "Let me try the lay-off again. It's fun."

Patrick laughed. He shook his head. "Lay*out*, Cindi, not layoff."

I blushed. "I know that," I said. I wondered why I had made the slip of the tongue.

I did the layout about twenty times on the trampoline. I discovered that in order to do it right, I had to have a lot of height. If I wasn't really flying I couldn't do it, but if I was high enough, I could just sail around with my body perfectly straight.

It was so much fun. There is nothing, *nothing*, like learning a new trick in gymnastics. Suddenly something that you could only watch someone else do becomes something that your body knows how to do. I love it. It's why gymnastics is never boring. You never do the same thing over and over.

The Stupidest Words in the English Language

"You were sensational," said Darlene when I finally took off the harness.

"You saw it?" I asked.

"Who could miss it?" teased Jodi. "You were flying over our heads all afternoon."

"It was a blast," I said. "It's called a layout twist."

"Who doesn't know that?" said Becky as we went into the locker room. "I mean, I can't believe you've been in gymnastics this long, and you didn't even know what a layout twist is."

"I knew," I said. Lauren winked at me. She always knows when I'm not quite telling the truth.

Lauren took my arm. "Don't let her bug you. She's just jealous 'cause you were so good."

"I was, wasn't I?" I admitted.

"Yeah," said Lauren. "You're just getting better and better," she said.

I blushed, but I knew it was true. Lately everything had started to click for me in gymnastics. It was an incredible feeling. I didn't even mind Becky being jealous. In fact, it made me proud. Ever since Heidi had started working out at our gym, all the Pinecones had taken giant leaps forward. When the competitions started in January we'd be able to give our archrivals, the Atomic Amazons, something to worry about.

I came out of practice just flying. Even Jared was impressed. Mom and Dad both picked us up, which is a little unusual, but I didn't have time to think about it.

As soon as we got into the car Jared started blabbing about me. "Mom, Dad, you will not believe what Cindi did on the trampoline today. She was so cool. She looked like Heidi Ferguson out there. Olympic caliber."

As much as Jared and I fight, it felt great that he was bragging about me.

"I'm not kidding," said Jared. "You were sensational."

I blushed. "Yeah, well, it's one thing to do it

on the trampoline, but it'll be months before I can try it as a dismount. The first time I did it just by mistake. Instead of doing a regular somersault, I kept my legs and body straight — see, that's called a layout, and . . ."

I stopped. Dad looked kind of uptight, and Mom was being really quiet.

"Is anything wrong?" I asked. "Mom, you're not talking." It wasn't like Mom not to talk. She's the real chatterbox of the family most of the time.

"What's up?" asked Jared.

"We'll talk when we get home," said Mom. "Let Dad concentrate on driving in the snow."

"Your mom and I have something to talk to you kids about," said Dad.

"Lauren always says that those are the scariest words in the English language," I blurted out.

"Which words?" asked Dad.

" 'There's something I want to talk to you about,' " I said.

Dad laughed. "She's right honey," he said, "but don't worry."

Jared and I leaned back in the rear seat of the car and looked at each other.

Jared shrugged.

"Is it something we did?" I asked Mom and Dad anxiously.

Dad shook his head. "Please, honey, don't worry."

I'd have to tell Lauren I had a new one for her. "There's something I want to talk to you about" might be the scariest words in the language, but "don't worry" are the stupidest.

7

Hip-Deep in Alligators

When we pulled into our driveway, there was already a car parked there, one covered with mud and dents.

"Steve's home!" yelled Jared. Steve is my brother who goes to the University of Colorado in Boulder.

We ran into the house. Steve and Tim were both there. Steve's about six feet three. He plays varsity football, and his forearms are about the size of my legs. He picked me up and gave me a hug.

Tim is sixteen, and he's much slighter than Steve, although he loves sports as much as anybody else in my family. His real love is music.

He's a bass guitar player, and he's just started a rock band.

"What is this?" I asked. "A family council? Everybody's here except Chris." Chris was in California where he was going to college.

"Steve, you didn't have to come back," said Dad.

"I wanted to," said Steve.

I looked at Mom and Dad. All I could think of was that Dad was really sick. Maybe he had a kind of cancer, and that was why Steve had come right home.

"Daddy, what's wrong?" I cried.

"Honey, it's nothing horrible," said Dad. "I've been laid off. I was pretty sure it was going to happen when my flights last week were canceled, but I just found out today for sure. The airline has been bought by another company, and they already have more pilots than they need. They're going to be cutting back on their lines."

"Laid off?" I repeated. "You mean, fired?"

"Well, technically, it's a layoff," said Dad. "It means that I could be called back to work if the new airline expands, but in this economy that's not very likely."

"I can't believe you didn't tell us," I said. I was furious. "You told Steve. . . . What were you waiting for — for us to read about it in the papers?"

"I told you as soon as I knew for sure. Rumors

about this have been in the papers for days now," said Dad. "It's been nothing but gossip for months. I didn't want to worry you before I had to. The rumors have been wrong so many times I thought this might be just another false alarm."

"Still, you and Mom have been talking about this, haven't you?" I accused them.

"We didn't and don't want you kids to panic," said Dad. "But we wanted you all together so we could talk about what's going to happen. It's scary, but we're going to get through this. Everything will be all right."

"What *is* going to happen, Dad?" asked Tim.

"I don't know," said Dad, rubbing his hand through his red hair. "Pilots will always be needed, and I'll get another job, but it might take a while. We've got some savings, and they'll pay me two months' salary in a lump sum. Everything will eventually get back to normal."

"I can quit college for a year," said Steve.

"No!" said Dad sharply. "Absolutely not. You're on partial scholarship. Chris is looking into financial aid. You're both staying in school."

"Things are going to be harder," said Mom. "And we'll need your help. But with everyone pitching in we can save a lot of money. Mostly your dad and I don't want you to worry. We'll just have to cut back on some things, like popcorn at the movies."

"Mom," said Tim, "cutting back on popcorn at the movies is not going to save a lot of money."

"I know," said Mom. "We won't be getting a new hot-water heater, right now. And we'll have to hope the car doesn't break down. We can't afford a new one, but it doesn't mean we won't still have good times."

"I can give up my electric bass lessons," said Tim. "I can still play with the school band and take lessons at school, but we can save on private lessons."

"Thanks, Tim," said Dad. "That'll be a help."

I stared at Tim. I knew how much he loved his electric bass teacher, a man who played in a great jazz band. Tim would hate giving up his lessons.

"I could quit gymnastics," said Jared. "I mean, I love hockey and football, too. And I can still play school sports. Then you wouldn't have to pay for my lessons."

I felt like everyone was looking at me.

"I'll quit gymnastics, too," I said.

Dad sighed. "Cindi, I really hate for you to do that — if there were any way that we could afford to keep sending you, we would."

I blinked. I don't think until that moment I believed that Dad was serious. I was sure he would say, "Honey, that's asking too much. We know you love gymnastics." But Dad didn't say that. He wasn't saying that at all.

Dad came over and put his arm around me. "With any luck we'll have both you and me flying again in the new year. It might just be for a little while."

"If there were any way we could have you continue with gymnastics we would," said Mom. "We know you love it."

"It's okay," I said. "I mean, like Jared . . . I'll still have sports at school."

My elementary school didn't have a gymnastics team, and it wouldn't be the same at all without Darlene, Lauren, Jodi, Ti An, even Ashley — without Patrick, Heidi, and Dimitri. I just felt numb. I couldn't believe it was happening.

"We're paid up at Patrick's until the end of next week," said Mom. "You can go until then."

"What about Christmas this year?" said Jared. "It's gonna be such a bummer."

"It won't," said Mom. "Your grandparents went through plenty of hard times, and they always said, 'If your problem is just about money, it can't be that bad.' "

Dad started to laugh. "Grandma and Grandpa are right," he said. "Although my dad used to say, 'When you're hip-deep in alligators it's hard to remember why they had to drain the swamp.' "

"Dad," I said, "that doesn't make any sense at all."

"It never did to me, either," said Dad. "But

neither does losing my job. The one thing I know is we've all got to keep *our* sense of humor and pull together. You kids are the greatest."

I bit my lip. I was trying hard not to cry. I didn't feel like the greatest, and I *hated, hated*, what was happening. I hated it with all my heart.

Here Come Those Frightening Words Again

I had trouble sleeping. I wanted to sleep. I kept thinking about what Mom had said, that this wasn't the worst thing in the world. But it was awful! I wouldn't be with my friends — my team! I wanted to take a huge eraser and wipe the whole thing out — make everything go back to the way it had been before. I wanted to make the airline rich again and force them to give Daddy back his job.

I knew that having to quit gymnastics wasn't like being homeless or having cancer — nobody would really feel sorry for a kid who had to quit gymnastics. It didn't rank up there with life's great tragedies. Nobody was going to make a TV movie-of-the-week about Cindi Jockett — a girl who has to take school gymnastics instead of private lessons.

Yet it was a big deal to me. And I felt so sad. I wouldn't be a Pinecone anymore — I wasn't going to be at the gym, and that's where we all belonged — together at the gym.

I woke up feeling as if all I wanted to do was pull the covers up over my head. On top of that, it was a gray day.

The sun never came out all day, and my mood never changed. I managed to make it through school without bawling, but I don't think I learned much. Lauren and Jodi both go to P.S. 64 with me. We're in the fifth grade, and we were studying how the native Americans lived in Colorado before Columbus. The oldest of these cultures, the Anasazi, built dwellings on top of each other along cliff walls. They were the biggest apartment houses in the world until the ones in New York City.

Everybody worked together. They shared everything. Maybe I should have been born an Anasazi. And then my dad wouldn't have lost his job.

I didn't say anything to anybody about Dad. I didn't want to talk about it. Every once in a while, Lauren would give me a kind of strange look, but I ignored her.

Finally, after school, she caught up with me.

"Want a ride over to the gym?" she asked me. "My mom's picking me up." Lauren's mom is on the city council. Her dad is a high school principal. They have two jobs and only one kid. It didn't seem fair.

I knew I had to tell Lauren. She is my best friend. I can't keep secrets from her. Pinecones just don't have secrets from one another.

I couldn't figure out exactly what to say.

Lauren's mother honked the horn. "Come on," said Lauren, grabbing my hand.

I let her drag me along. We piled into the Bacas' car. "Hi, Mom," said Lauren, giving her mom a kiss. Everything was so normal for Lauren. It made me mad. I sank into the corner of the backseat.

Jodi got in next to me. Lauren turned around in the front to face us.

"Put on your seat belt," said Mrs. Baca.

"Okay, okay," said Lauren. "Cindi, it was so weird — just now I flashed back to our very first day. Remember, you dragged me to this new gym you heard about, the Evergreen Gymnastics Academy. I thought I was going to hate it."

I stared out the window and bit my lip. Lauren turned around. "I don't know what made me think of that right now," she said.

"Yeah," I said, "we had daydreams about going to the Olympics. What a joke!"

"It's not such a joke," said Jodi. "I'll bet Heidi's going to go — maybe she'll take the Pinecones with her. We're her good luck charm, remember?"

I didn't say anything. When the Olympics came I'd be long gone as a Pinecone. The closest I would get would be to watch Heidi and the Pinecones on television.

We pulled up in front of the gym. It had started to snow again; not the big, fluffy flakes that are so pretty — these were more like ice pellets.

"I hate winter," said Jodi. We ran into the gym.

In the locker room, I kept looking at things, thinking that I'd never see them again. *My* locker — it would belong to somebody else. I wanted to put a huge padlock on it and a sign that read DO NOT USE — EVER.

"Will you look at this?" shouted Becky. She had a piece of paper in her hand. "I don't believe it!"

"What's your problem now?" asked Darlene.

"Patrick and Dimitri made up a flier for the Holiday Show, and they got it all wrong," cried Becky.

"Did they forget to tell people it's for the Save the Evergreen Fund?" asked Lauren, sounding worried.

"No," said Becky. "But they don't mention me anywhere!"

"Let me see that," said Darlene.

I barely listened. It all sounded so silly — fighting about who got credit for the Holiday Show. I wouldn't even be there for the show.

Becky thrust the paper at Darlene. " 'The Evergreen Gymnastics Academy invites you to celebrate the holidays with us. Our students will put on a show that will have you on the edge of your seats — and all proceeds will go to the Save the Evergreen Fund,' " she read.

"I think it sounds great," said Jodi. "I like the 'edge of the seat' part."

"It should have mentioned that it was Becky Dyson's idea," pouted Becky. "I told all my parents' friends to come."

I rolled my eyes. "She is one thing I will not miss," I said as I closed my locker.

Darlene heard me. "What does that mean?" she asked.

I knew I couldn't keep the bad news to myself much longer. My teammates deserved to know the truth.

"Wait till Becky leaves," I said to Darlene. "I've got something to say to the Pinecones."

Darlene and Lauren looked at each other. They both looked worried. I hadn't realized it, but I had just said some of those frightening words again: "There's something I've got to talk to you about."

Don't Look Back

The Pinecones gathered around my locker —
Darlene, Lauren, Jodi, Ti An, and Ashley.

"I'm quitting gymnastics," I said. "I can't take
gymnastics anymore."

"Very funny," said Lauren. "This is not April
Fool's Day, remember. It's getting close to Christmas."

"My dad lost his job," I said. "I've *got* to quit.
We can't afford it."

There was dead silence for several moments.
"I wanted you all to be the first to know," I said.
"I didn't want you to have to find out from any-
body else."

"You're serious," whispered Lauren.
I nodded.

"This is *so* sad," said Ti An.

Jodi looked like she was having a hard time believing it. "Wait a minute. Maybe you're exaggerating. I bet your parents don't want you to quit. They'll find the money somewhere."

"Jodi," I said to her. "Chris and Steve were thinking about dropping out of college. That's a little more important than gymnastics."

"Well, yeah," admitted Lauren, "but — "

"Forget it," I said. "We'd better go out to the gym. I have to tell Patrick."

"Patrick!" said Jodi, as if she were a cartoon character with a light bulb going off in her head. "He'll figure out a way to let you stay." The Pinecones all started muttering at once. They were absolutely convinced that Patrick would be able to do something that would let me stay.

"Patrick wouldn't break up the Pinecones," said Ti An, sounding as if she had been a Pinecone all her life, when it hadn't really been so long ago that she had joined us.

I tried not to get my hopes up, but as we walked into the gym, I swear the sun came out, and I could see streaks of sunlight coming through the skylight.

The Pinecones formed a circle around me as we walked over to Patrick, who was talking with Heidi and Dimitri.

Patrick glanced up at me, and I knew right

away that he already knew about my dad.

"Patrick," said Darlene, "there's something we've got to talk to you about."

Now it was Patrick's turn to look a little worried. It was like a strange game of telephone or hot potato. The same phrase kept being passed around.

I was glad that it was Darlene who had decided to speak first. She the oldest Pinecone. She's our captain, and I trust her.

"I think I know what you're going to say," said Patrick. "And I don't blame you for being upset. Cindi, I'm so sorry about this."

"You know that Cindi has to quit gymnastics?" Lauren asked, her voice going up an octave.

Patrick nodded. "Cindi, your dad called me today. He explained the situation. He wanted me to give him some exercises that you could do. He wants to help you stay in shape, and he said that as soon as he finds a job, you'll be back."

I gritted my teeth. It was awful that Dad had already called Patrick. Somehow that made it so final — so real.

"Patrick!" shrieked Lauren. "You've *got* to do something! You can't let Cindi leave."

"I wish she didn't have to," said Patrick. "And, Cindi, I hope with all my heart that you'll be back."

My face felt like it was on fire.

I hadn't realized how much I had been hoping that Patrick would say something that would make everything all right. But he didn't. All he was saying was that he was sorry.

I didn't need him sorry.

"It's okay," I said stiffly. "It's not as if it's the end of the world."

The Pinecones all turned to me. "It'll be terrible without you," said Jodi.

Patrick put his arm around me, but I moved away.

"It's okay," I repeated. "It's not your fault, Patrick."

But that's not the way I felt.

"Cindi, I wish we weren't such a small gym here. I wish I had the money to pay for your lessons myself. I feel terrible. But you're going to be back. It's happened before that girls have had to leave for a short time, and they've come back better than ever. I'll give you a great set of exercises so that you can stay in terrific shape."

Patrick took one look at my face. "I know this feels awful." He didn't. Nobody knew how terrible it felt. I hated people saying that.

"Patrick," wailed Lauren, "isn't there something you can do?"

He sighed. "Lauren, there are some things that

are beyond our control. This is one of those things."

"But . . . but . . ." stammered Lauren.

"Please," I begged them, "will you all stop talking about this? You're making me sick."

I ran out of the gym and back into the locker room. I stuffed my things into my gym bag and put on my street clothes. Heidi came in after me.

"Cindi," she said, "I just heard. I'm so sorry."

"I don't need your pity," I snapped. "I don't need anybody's pity."

"I . . . I don't know what to say," sputtered Heidi. "I just wanted you to know that I know how you must feel."

I closed my eyes, hoping that I wouldn't explode. Heidi came from a rich family, and she was so talented that people were lined up to try to help her get into the Olympics. She did *not* know how I felt.

"I'll be fine," I said.

"Yeah, well, keep in shape," said Heidi awkwardly.

I grabbed a quarter and called home. Luckily Tim answered the phone.

"Pick me up at the gym *now!*" I said to him urgently.

"It's only four," said Tim. "Don't you have practice until five-thirty?"

"*Now*," I repeated. "I told everybody and now they're all feeling sorry for me. I can't stand it."

"I know how you feel," said Tim. "I had to tell my jazz teacher today that I couldn't take any more lessons. I'll be there in fifteen minutes." At least Tim *did* know how I felt.

"Thanks," I said.

I put on my snow boots and parka and went outside.

Patrick came after me. "Cindi wait," he called, sounding out of breath, "you can't leave like this."

"How do you want me to leave?" I asked him. "Would you rather wait until I was crying?"

I wiped my nose on my parka sleeve. I was *that* close to bawling.

Patrick blinked. "Cindi, I am so sorry," he said. "I want you to always feel that you've got a home here. You can call me if you want to talk about anything. And I'd like you to come back here for the next two weeks — and stay through the Holiday Show. Maybe by then things will have changed."

I shook my head. "Patrick, I can't," I said. "It hurts too much. I'd rather just leave — please? If I stayed it would just feel worse, and if I leave now, you can refund my parents the money for the next couple of weeks."

Patrick sighed. "Of course. Cindi, you know I'm here for you if you need me."

I nodded. I knew Patrick cared, but he couldn't really help. It would be awful to stay and do the Holiday Show and then have to leave forever. It was better to make a clean break.

Thank goodness it wasn't long before I heard a car horn honk. I've never been so relieved to see Tim in my life.

I bolted from Patrick and grabbed the car door.

Tim looked at me. "Tough, huh," he said. "Did you tell him about Dad?"

I nodded. "He knew. Dad called him. Everybody's feeling sorry for me. I hate it."

"I know," said Tim. "It was the same way with my jazz teacher. He felt really bad."

I couldn't talk. I burst out crying.

Tim patted my arm. I turned and through my tears I realized that Patrick was still standing there in front of the gym.

"Drive," I said. "Get me out of here."

Tim put the car in gear, and we drove off. I couldn't look back.

10

Things Couldn't Get Worse

Mom and Dad said that they understood why I felt I had to quit the gym "cold turkey."

"What good would it do to keep going?" I asked. "I'd just know that I couldn't go back."

Dad nodded. "As soon as we can, we'll get you back with the Pinecones," he said. And that was all he said about the subject.

Dad had enough troubles of his own. I didn't want to worry him, but I missed the Pinecones so much. I couldn't talk to anybody about it because I didn't want anyone to feel sorry for me.

The sky didn't fall when I stopped going to gymnastics. I did my exercises, sit-ups and push-ups. But it was boring.

By Saturday, after a week without gynmastics,

a week without my team, I was jumping out of my skin. I wandered downstairs.

Mom and Dad were sitting at the kitchen table with a bunch of pipe cleaners spread out.

"What are those for?" I asked.

"They were left over from an old course in crafts that I took," said Mom. "I'm making Christmas ornaments. I needed to do something."

I picked up Mom's book. *The Crafty You: Saving Money With Crafts.*

"The 'Crafty You'?" I teased. Mom is not the arts-and-crafts type. She likes going to crafts fairs, but she's not very good at making things.

"Every little bit helps," said Dad. I couldn't believe he was playing with pipe cleaners. The phone rang. Dad got up to answer it.

I sank down into a kitchen chair next to Mom. She glanced at me. "Remember, honey," she said, "things are going to get better."

I sighed. It seemed that was *all* Mom was saying lately. I was getting sick of people telling me things were going to get better. "Are we going to be saying that every day?" I asked.

Mom laughed. "I guess I have been repeating myself a little."

"A little," I teased her.

"I'm sorry you're so sad, Cindi," said Mom. "I think it might be hardest on you, 'cause you're the youngest."

I didn't want Mom to think I needed to be babied. "It's okay, Mom, honest. It's just that I miss the Pinecones — I miss the gym, but I'm doing my exercises."

"It's hard on everybody," said Mom. "We're all making sacrifices."

I didn't want to tell Mom I thought leaving the Pinecones was a *huge* sacrifice.

Mom gave me a hug. I hugged her back. "It's not *so* bad," she said. "We've got some savings. I'm being honest with you, Cindi. I don't think these hard times are going to last. Things *will* get better. And there are a lot of people much worse off than we are."

I was getting a little tired of hearing that, too, but I nodded. Dad hung up the phone. "That was the guy from the union," he said. "He can see us today to go over our health benefits."

"Good," said Mom. "Cindi, we have to go out for a little while, but Tim and Jared are here."

"Mom, I'm eleven years old, remember? You don't have to worry about leaving me alone."

"I know," said Mom. "It's just that you'll always be the baby of the family. I can't help myself."

"Yeah, right," I said. After Mom and Dad left I stared at the pipe cleaners spread out on the table. I found them depressing. I started to clean them up, and I took a bunch of them and stuck them in my pocket. Maybe I'd make my own presents this year. I sure didn't have much money in my allowance to spend on presents. I went upstairs.

Tim's door was open. He used to share a room with Jared before Steve and Chris went off to college. Tim had earphones on. I went into his room and pulled the earphones off. He turned around, looking annoyed.

"Sorry," I said.

"What's up?" he asked. "I'm doing my homework."

Jared walked by. "Is the twerp bothering you?" he asked.

"Don't call me a twerp," I blurted out, but my heart wasn't into fighting with Jared.

"It is just so weird to be coming home from school every day instead of going to the gym. I miss my team."

"I know, it stinks," said Tim. "I miss my jazz lessons, but what can you do?"

"I wish I could afford to pay for my own lessons at the gym," I said.

"Cindi, you're eleven. You can't get a job."

"I could try to get more baby-sitting jobs," I said.

"That's a good idea," said Tim. "Now, can I get back to my homework?"

"Except that most of the people I baby-sit for are cutting back on going out, too," I said. "I haven't had many calls lately."

"Cindi," said Tim, "we all know things are tough. It doesn't help to dwell on it."

"Yeah, Cindi-rella, lighten up," said Jared.

"Don't call me that," I said. "I *hate* that name."

Jared stuck his tongue out at me.

"Don't tease her," said Tim. "We're all in lousy moods. We shouldn't take it out on each other."

"All she does is mope," said Jared.

"Jared . . ." warned Tim.

"Okay, okay," said Jared. "Anyhow, I've got things to do."

Jared turned and left.

"I'm sorry I disturbed you," I said to Tim.

Tim shrugged. "What *is* on your mind?"

"This is going to be such a crummy Christmas," I said. "I can't stand it. Mom and Dad are going to try to pretend that everything's normal, but it isn't."

Tim turned in his chair. "Yo, Cindi," he said, "this isn't you."

"What do you mean?" I asked.

"You don't usually just sit around and sulk. Why don't you *do* something? Or at least let me study."

I sighed. "I guess I do sound like a spoiled turkey."

"Somehow that's a disgusting image," said Tim.

I heard the doorbell ring.

"I'll get it," Jared yelled.

"Wow, Big Beef! I heard Jared say. "Hi, Darlene."

"What are Darlene and Big Beef doing here?" I whispered to Tim.

"They're your friends," said Tim. "It's not as if you've got leprosy or something. Why shouldn't they be here?"

"Hey, Cindi-rella," Jared shouted up the stairs, "you've got company."

I licked my lips. Suddenly I felt so nervous. There was nothing to be nervous about. Things couldn't get worse.

11

Learning About Pride

I went downstairs. Big Beef was taking off his snow boots, and Cleo was sniffing them as if she had never seen anything that huge.

"Cleo, come back here," I said. Cleo just wagged her tail a little to acknowledge that I had spoken, but she ignored me.

"Cleo!" I said, a little more sharply. I grabbed her collar and pulled her away.

"Hi, Cindi," said Darlene. She sounded a little shy. She reached down and patted Cleo on the head. I had seen Jodi and Lauren every day at school, but I hadn't seen Darlene for a whole week.

"Hi, Darlene," I said. "You look good." She was wearing a red sweater with a black-and-purple design on it, and black velvet leggings.

"Thanks," said Darlene. We looked at each other. We were sounding so polite, as if we hardly knew each other.

"How're things at the gym?" I asked.

Darlene shrugged. "Becky's still just as much of a pain as ever," she said.

"That's one person I don't miss," I said.

Big Beef stood around in his stocking feet, shifting his weight. It occurred to me that it was a bit strange that he had taken his boots off in the first place. I had figured Big Beef had just driven Darlene over to say hello, but if that was the case, what was he doing with his boots off? Suddenly I was as curious about those big boots as Cleo.

Darlene started smiling.

"What?" I asked. I know Darlene's looks. She was bursting to tell me something.

"Uh, Cindi, is your mom or dad home?" asked Big Beef. "There's something I want to talk to your family about."

"Uh-oh," I said. "It's catching."

Big Beef looked at me curiously. "What?" he asked.

"Nothing," I said. I didn't want to explain about what those words had come to mean to me. "Sorry," I said. "Mom and Dad went out for a while. I think they'll be back soon."

"I knew we should have called before we came over," said Big Beef, "but Darlene just couldn't wait."

"Dad," protested Darlene, "you're not being fair. This is about Cindi, not her parents."

Big Beef sighed. Then he smiled. He's got a great, huge smile. "Sorry, girls," said Big Beef. "I think we'd better wait until Cindi's folks come home."

Tim came down the stairs. He shook hands with Big Beef. "I can't believe you're actually in our house," said Tim. "Wait till my brother Steve hears about this. He's on a football scholarship at the University of Colorado."

"I know," said Big Beef. "I've heard about him from Cindi, and he's building quite a reputation for himself."

Tim grinned. "Yeah, well, he keeps saying that if he does get to be a pro player then he'll come home and bring the Broncos to the Super Bowl."

"Hey, wait a minute," said Big Beef. "We've still got a chance for a wild-card place in the play-offs this year. Don't count us out."

I coughed. I was too anxious to find out what Big Beef wanted to just stand around and talk football.

"Dad," exploded Darlene, "you're driving me crazy! Please, can't we tell Cindi what we decided to do?"

Big Beef shook his head. Jared, Tim, and I looked at each other. It was so mysterious.

Finally we heard the garage door open. "Mom and Dad are home, I think," I said.

"Good," said Big Beef.

"What's this about?" I whispered to Darlene.

Darlene blew air in her cheeks. "I'd better let Dad tell you," she said.

I couldn't stand the suspense.

I heard Mom and Dad in the kitchen. "Mom, Dad!" I yelled. "We've got company!"

Mom and Dad came into the front room. Big Beef stuck out his hand and shook theirs. "Sorry to barge in on you," he said. "Darlene insisted on my coming right over. We should have called."

"That's okay," said Dad. "It's good to see you. What can I do for you?"

"Maybe I should talk to you privately," said Big Beef.

"Dad," protested Darlene. "That's not fair. It's about *Cindi*."

My father looked at Tim and Jared. "If it's about Cindi," said Dad, "boys, why don't you leave us alone?"

Jared and Tim both looked annoyed that they couldn't stay with Big Beef, but they went upstairs.

Big Beef waited until they were gone. Then he looked at me. He seemed a little awkward, and it struck me funny that such a big grown-up would act awkward. "When Darlene told me how much the Pinecones missed you, Cindi, I really felt bad about it. You know, I've always thought I've been very lucky, and that life's not fair." Big Beef looked at my dad, who nodded at him.

"Right now in my work, football, there's a lot of money, and I get paid a big salary — and in your field, at the airlines, there isn't a lot of work," continued Big Beef. "Darlene tells me the Pinecones aren't doing very well without Cindi, and I know this may be uncomfortable for you, but since life's not fair, and Darlene tells me that money's tight for you . . . I'd like to offer whatever it costs to keep Cindi in the Pinecones until you get your job back."

"Boy, is that nice," said my dad.

I looked at him. It was really nice, but it was *really* embarrassing. My face felt as red as my hair.

"It is," I said, but I felt so strange.

Dad sighed. "I wish that I could just say, Thanks, we'll take your money," said Dad. He glanced at Mom. She nodded. Then they both looked at me.

"It's okay, Dad," I said. Somehow I knew even before Dad said anything that we couldn't let Big Beef pay for my lessons.

"I cannot tell you how much I appreciate your

offer," Dad said to Big Beef. "But as much as I want Cindi to be back in the Pinecones, I have to say no, and thank you. I just have too many loans, and I couldn't pay you back, and that would make me feel uncomfortable."

"Big Beef," said Mom, "It's the kindest offer in the whole world, but . . ." Her voice trailed off. I made a face. I hated Mom and Dad having to sound so apologetic.

"I understand," said Big Beef, "but I just wanted to let you know I'd be willing to do this."

Dad shook Big Beef's hand. "It was a great offer," he said. "I thank you."

Big Beef started to put on his boots. "I don't blame you for turning me down. We shouldn't have sprung it on you, but Darlene couldn't wait. If you want to talk it over and give me a call, you can. Come on, Darlene."

"I don't get it," said Darlene. "I thought this would make everything okay."

"It's just not that easy," I tried to explain.

"You're not mad at me, are you?" Darlene asked worriedly.

I shook my head. "It was terrific of you," I said.

Dad nodded. "Believe me," he said, "it's the nicest thing that's happened to us in a long time."

Dad put his arm around me. I was proud of my dad. In a very weird way, it would have made me feel bad to take Big Beef's money. I guess I was learning about pride. But it wasn't easy. These lessons in pride were harder than anything I had had to learn in gymnastics. These lessons hurt.

Walking on Eggs

I walked down the school corridor hugging my notebook to my chest. I couldn't wait until Christmas vacation, which was just a week away. I wanted to say "forget it" to my whole world. "I'm outta here."

I felt a tug on my arm. I turned around. It was Lauren.

"Hi," I said.

"You've been ignoring me," accused Lauren.

"No, I haven't. I've been busy," I said. "Come on, Lauren. We'll be late for class."

"You never say more than ten words to me," complained Lauren. "It's always, hi, good-bye, or have to go to class — see you later."

"It's a proven fact that's eleven words," I said.

Lauren made a face. "Very cute," she said. "You've been acting as if I don't exist."

"That's not true," I protested, although I knew exactly what Lauren was talking about. I hadn't meant to hurt Lauren's feelings, but it hurt me too much to be around her. Every time I saw her, I was sure she was feeling sorry for me. "We see each other every day in school," I argued.

"The Pinecones *all* want to see you," said Lauren. "They want to know if we can visit you today after we get out of gymnastics."

I looked suspicious. "Did Darlene tell you what her father offered to do?" I asked Lauren.

Lauren nodded. "She wasn't supposed to," she said, "but it just came out."

I understood. The Pinecones never had secrets from each other.

"You aren't coming over with another scheme to pay for my lessons, are you?" I asked Lauren.

"You really are a hard case," said Lauren. "Everybody just misses you, but they were afraid that you'd bite their heads off."

"Am I really that bad?" I asked Lauren.

Lauren shrugged. "Kind of," she said.

"Are Darlene and Big Beef mad at me?" I asked Lauren.

She shook her head. "Absolutely not. Darlene

said Big Beef told her that he would probably have reacted in the same way. He said he thought he went about it in the wrong way."

"It was really nice of him to offer," I said. "I mean it."

Jodi came up to us in the hall. "Did you ask her about our coming over today?" she said to Lauren.

"She was about to say okay," said Lauren.

"I can't believe you guys thought you needed a formal invitation," I said. Nothing had made me feel so much like an outsider.

"You've been acting like you don't want to have anything to do with us," said Jodi.

"That's not true," I said.

"Great," said Jodi. "So we'll see you after practice. Around five-thirty."

"Yeah," I said. "Super great."

Jodi checked to see if I was being sarcastic, but I wasn't trying to be.

Jared had basketball practice after school, so I went home on the bus without him.

Cleo was glad to see me when I got home, but she was alone. The house smelled of chili. It was lucky we all liked it and that Mom and Dad made it so delicious. We had been eating chili a lot lately. There was a note from Mom on the refrigerator, saying that she was out until dinner. I knew that Tim was probably still at school. He doesn't ever get home from high school before five o'clock.

I heard sounds from the basement, and for a second I got scared. "Hi, honey," said Dad as he popped his head into the kitchen.

"I forgot you were home," I exclaimed. I immediately felt guilty. Of course Dad would be home. Where else would he be?

"I'm just working on the hot-water heater down in the basement," said Dad. "It's better than just moping around, and maybe I can actually fix it. I like keeping my hands busy." He got a drink of water. "How was school today?"

"Fine," I said. "The Pinecones are coming over here after their practice, just to say hello."

"That's great," said Dad. "I'll be really happy to see them. I miss them, too."

I knew Dad meant it, but I didn't think he would ever understand how much *I* missed the Pinecones. "Sure," I said. "Well, I'm going upstairs. I've got homework."

I didn't have homework. I had finished my homework in study hall. I just didn't want to stay downstairs. Each word seemed to just hang in the air, waiting. Nothing felt normal around our house anymore. We were all walking on eggs, worried about saying the wrong thing.

I went up to my room. The pipe cleaners were still out on my desk. I couldn't think of a thing to do, and I had two whole hours to waste before the Pinecones came to visit. They had gymnastics in the afternoon, and all I had was free time.

13

Pinecones for the Pinecones

I got Mom's book on crafts. Maybe it *was* time for me to quit moping around and do something to help.

"The natural look in crafts is 'in,' " I read in the book. "Don't overlook the free materials just waiting for you in your own backyard."

I looked out at our backyard. The ground was covered with snow. There was a big blue spruce in the corner, but I don't think Mom or Dad would have liked it if I cut it down to sell it as a Christmas tree.

"Try making a basket of twigs and pinecones for the holiday season," said the book. "Nothing could be easier, especially if you use the modern pipe cleaner to help hold things together. Don't look for perfection. It's the little imperfections that will make your craft special."

"Hmmm," I said out loud. I sighed. Pinecones. It was as if I was never going to get away from that word. Still, maybe it was a sign. Maybe I'd create something so beautiful everyone would want one.

I put on my boots and went outside. There was a crust on the snow, and it made crunching sounds as I walked on it. Cleo followed me, but she was light enough so that she didn't fall through the crust.

The sun was low in the sky, making deep shadows on the snow. I gathered a bunch of twigs and pinecones and brought them back to the house. I spread them out on the kitchen table.

"There," I said to Cleo. "We've got everything for a beautiful basket, and it didn't cost us anything."

Cleo looked a little doubtful. The book said to soak the twigs in warm water so that they would bend, and to make the base out of pipe cleaners.

I started to work.

I was still working when the doorbell rang. I ran to get it with a dripping twig in my hand.

It was all the Pinecones: Darlene, Lauren, Cindi, Ti An, and Ashley.

"You're not eating bark, are you?" asked Ti An. "At school we're studying how the Native Americans had to eat tree bark when the white man killed off all the buffalo."

I laughed. "No, Ti An, we're not eating bark. Come on in. I'm making a basket."

Darlene gave me a look. "Basket weaving?" she asked.

"What's wrong with that?" I asked her.

"Nothing," said Darlene. "It's just that you hate crafts."

I showed the Pinecones into the kitchen. There were pinecones and twigs lying all over. I had the wet twigs in the sink.

"The chili smells great," said Darlene. I got her a spoon so she could have a taste. I gave Lauren a bowl. I know that Lauren loves my folks' chili.

"Is this a basket?" asked Ti An. She held my basket up to the light. I hadn't noticed there was a big hole in the bottom of it.

Ti An's little face was peering out through the bottom. Lauren giggled. I started to laugh a little, too. Crafts were definitely not my thing.

"I'll fix it," said Ti An. She grabbed a bunch of pipe cleaners and began to weave a bottom to the basket. She took some of the twigs out of the bucket and wound them around the pipe cleaners.

"You make it look so easy," I groaned. Ti An kept working. "How're things at the gym?" I asked, trying to keep my voice level.

"Patrick's getting lots of little kids for the Tiny Tots program," said Jodi. "They're taking over the gym. They're everywhere. It's like a fungus."

Jodi's mom just had a baby — Travis is Jodi's half brother, and Jodi likes to pretend that she hates having him around. But I think she's just faking it. Actually, she's kind of proud of him.

"Here," said Ti An. She handed me the basket. It actually didn't look bad — at least the part that Ti An had worked on. My part had twigs that stuck straight out. It looked like half basket, half porcupine. "You could fill it with pinecones," suggested Ti An. "Then it would look great for the holidays."

"Are you giving it to your mom for Christmas?" Ashley asked me.

"I was thinking of trying to sell them," I said, looking a little doubtful.

"Sell it?" guffawed Ashley. The other Pinecones shot her a dirty look, but she was right.

"How long did it take you to make this one?" asked Darlene.

"A couple of hours," I admitted.

The Pinecones were silent. I rolled my eyes. I picked up a pinecone and a pipe cleaner and started nervously twisting the pipe cleaner around the pinecone.

"This is hopeless," I said. "It's so depressing. Everything I try to do is such a joke."

"What else have you tried?" asked Darlene.

"Nothing," I admitted. I took the pinecone and threw it through a basketball hoop we have over the wastepaper basket.

"Hey," said Ti An, rescuing it from the floor. "I think that's cruelty to a pinecone."

"No disrespect intended," I said.

Ti An started playing with the pipe cleaners around the pinecone.

Darlene closed Mom's crafts book. "I think you should try something you're good at," she said. "That's what my dad always says, that you should go from strengths."

"What strengths? I'm a good gymnast, and unless you're as good as Heidi Ferguson there's not much money in that."

"Look what I made," said Ti An. She had added pipe cleaner arms and legs to the pinecone, and she had bent the legs so it looked like it was doing a split.

"It's a Pinecone-Pinecone Gymnast," said Ti An.

"It's adorable," I said.

"It would make a cute ornament for a Christmas tree, wouldn't it?" said Lauren, taking it from Ti An. "You could make it with red and green pipe cleaners for Christmas. I bet you'd sell a lot of them. Little pinecone gymnasts for Christmas."

"Aggghhh," I said. "No way. Darlene was right. Crafts is not my strong suit."

"Can I keep it then?" asked Ti An.

"Sure," I said. "Pinecones belong with Pine-cones."

"You'll always be a Pinecone," said Lauren loyally.

I didn't want to depress my friends, so I kept quiet, but I knew it wasn't true. Everybody was playing a game of pretend. We were all pretending that nothing was different. But it was. I didn't want to see any more pinecones, either the real kind or the gymnasts. They only made me sad.

14

So Mad I
Could Spit

I remember a fairy tale I once read in which the moral was: Be careful what you wish for because it might come true.

I'd said I was sick of pinecones, and pretty soon the only ones I saw were on the ground under our spruce tree.

Oh, I saw Jodi and Lauren in school, and we were friendly, but they seemed to sense that I didn't really want to hear what was going on in the gym. Without that in common, we just didn't seem to have much to talk about.

It was a Saturday, the week before Christmas, and Dad still didn't have a job. I heard Mom and Dad saying that the entire airline might go bankrupt. Just what we needed — more gloomy news. I went up to my room to do some homework. I was spending an awful lot of time up in my room alone.

Tim and Jared knocked on my door.

"Hey, Cindi," said Tim, "do you want to go to the mall with us? I have to do some Christmas shopping, and Jared wants to come."

"Are we still having Christmas?" I asked.

Tim rolled his eyes. "No, we figured we should all sulk in our rooms on Christmas day — like you."

"I'm not sulking," I protested.

"You could have fooled me," said Tim.

I got worried. "Do Mom and Dad think I've been pouting?" I asked him.

Tim shook his head. "They've got their own problems but, yeah, they're worried about you."

"I tried making 'crafty' presents," I said. "I even thought of selling them. They were a joke."

"Crafts aren't your thing," said Tim. "Even when you were little you used to make the ugliest drawings in kindergarten."

"Thanks," I said.

"Just telling the truth," said Tim.

"I've still got some money left from my allowance," I said. "Maybe I will come with you to the mall. I'd like to get Mom and Dad something really nice this year."

"It doesn't have to be expensive to be nice," said Tim.

" 'And things will get better,' " I said, parroting the words that got said around our house at least once a day.

Tim laughed. Tim asked Mom and Dad if he could borrow the car for the afternoon, and we took off for the mall. Just driving in the same direction as the gym made me wish I were going to do gymnastics. I'd always pick gymnastics over shopping.

When we got to the mall, instead of going down the little access road to the Evergreen Gymnastics Academy, we turned into the parking lot. We parked near the Christmas tree. "Let's split up," said Tim. "We'll meet in an hour at Wacky Tacos, okay? I don't want either of you guys around."

"Well, I don't want to get stuck with Cindi," protested Jared.

"I don't need a baby-sitter." I got out of the car and slammed the door shut.

"Yeah, well, if you stay in such a rotten mood, nobody's going to get you a present," Jared shouted after me.

"Give her a break, will you?" I heard Tim say to Jared.

The mall was piping Christmas carols over

the loudspeakers. "See you in an hour," Tim told me.

I walked into the mall. I hate malls. I never know what to look at first. It was bad enough in good times, but now it seemed like it was full of people with nothing to do except spend money, and I didn't have any.

I told myself to calm down. I thought about getting Mom some bubble bath. She loves special things for her bath, and I remembered that there was a bath shop somewhere on the second floor.

I headed for the escalator. I've got a terrible sense of direction, and I'm always losing my way in the mall. It seems to me like the darned places are designed so that you'll just wander around forever.

I got to the top of the escalator and stopped dead in my tracks. A big lady in a green down jacket barreled into me, and so did her two kids.

"Hey, girlie, that's no place to stop!" shouted the lady.

I tried to move out of her way, but it was as if there was glue on my feet.

I couldn't believe what I was seeing. My face got red-hot.

About twenty feet from the top of the escalator was a little booth — like the kind you always see in the mall where people are collecting clothes for the homeless or some other worthwhile cause. But this booth was definitely, *definitely,* not for a worthwhile cause.

In bright red letters so big that nobody could miss them were the words KEEP CINDI JOCKETT IN GYMNASTICS.

I was so mad I could spit.

15

Something I Have To Do Alone

I felt so embarrassed. I stormed over there. There were a dozen little pinecone gymnast ornaments spread out on the booth. "What's going on?" I demanded.

Ti An and Lauren were talking to a lady with gray hair. She was pretty old, kind of bent over the way some old people are, and she didn't look like she had much money. Her coat was made out of cheap cloth that I was sure wasn't very warm.

"These are so cute," said the lady. "My granddaughter loves gymnastics."

"And it's for a good cause," said Ti An.

"Ti An!" I hissed.

"Shh," said Lauren. "We're making a sale."

"I'm sure your granddaughter will love one," said Darlene.

"In fact, more than one," added Jodi.

"Well," said the woman, "I don't think I want more than one. Who is Cindi Jockett, anyway? Is she crippled? Is this part of the Special Olympics?"

I thought I was going to die right then and there. Lauren tried to shoo me away. "Oh, she's a poor, unfortunate gymnast who's fallen on hard times," said Jodi.

My mouth fell open.

The woman started to open her change purse. "How much are they?" she asked.

"Two dollars and fifty cents," said Jodi. "A lot of work goes into each one."

The lady hesitated. I couldn't stand it. I grabbed one of the ornaments.

"Excuse me, ma'am, we'd like you to have this one for your granddaughter," I said. "It's free."

"Cindi!" muttered Lauren. "What are you doing?"

"Hush up," I warned Lauren. Lauren started to protest, and then she took one look at my face and realized that I meant business. She shut up.

"Free?" asked the woman.

"Yes," I said through clenched teeth. "You're the one-hundredth customer. You get one free."

"One-hundredth?" said Ti An. "She's only our fourth customer, and we've been here three hours."

"Ti An . . ." I warned her.

The woman had the little ornament in her hand and was looking very confused. She started to put the ornament down. I took her hand and folded it around the ornament. "Please," I said.

"Are you the unfortunate Cindi?" she asked. "I don't get it."

"My dad won the lottery last night. My friends just didn't know. I'll be fine."

The woman gave me a little smile, but she still looked mighty confused. Finally she walked away.

I saw a shopping bag. I started to push all the ornaments into it.

"What are you doing?" shrieked Lauren.

"I'm closing up this charity," I said.

Ti An climbed on the booth to help me. "Wow! I can't believe your dad won the lottery. That is so cool. Just when you needed it most."

"Ti An," said Darlene, "I don't think Cindi's father won the lottery."

"He didn't?" asked Ti An. I shook my head.

I looked up at the banner. I wanted to crumple it up, but I stopped myself.

"How could you guys do this?" I begged them.

Darlene shrugged. "We didn't know what to do," she said. "We wanted to do something. We missed you so much."

"I miss you, too," I said. "But I'm not a charity case — "

"I know that," said Lauren. "Are you sure *you* do?"

"Huh?!" I exploded. I couldn't believe what Lauren had just said. "What in the world are you saying?"

"At least we tried something to get you back in gymnastics," said Lauren. "What are *you* doing?"

I swallowed hard. "It's not my fault we don't have the money," I said.

"I'm not saying that," said Lauren. She held out her hand and ticked off points on her fingers. "But you won't take money from Big Beef. You get mad when *we* tried to raise money for you. It's like you just don't care."

"I do care!" I protested.

"Then do something about it!" shouted Lauren. A dozen shoppers turned around to see what the commotion was. A security guard came over. He looked up at the banner.

"What's going on here?" he asked. "Who's Cindi Jockett?"

"I am," I admitted.

"It's a very unofficial charity," I said. I climbed up on the booth and took down the banner. I didn't crumple it. I folded it up. I read the words KEEP CINDI JOCKETT IN GYMNASTICS. Lauren was right. The Pinecones had tried to help me, but what had I done for myself? I had to do something.

"We're just leaving," I said to the security guard. He nodded and walked away, satisfied.

"Where are we going?" Ti An asked me as she folded up the card table.

"Not we," I said. "Me." I turned to Lauren. "You were right. I'm going to talk to Patrick. Maybe there is something I can do for myself." I looked at my watch. "I'm supposed to meet Tim and Jared at Wacky Tacos in a half hour. Will you go there for me and tell them to pick me up at the gym?"

"The gym!" exclaimed Jodi. "Do you want us to go with you?"

I shook my head.

"Do you want a chicken or a beef taco?" asked Lauren.

"I'm not hungry," I said. I was excited. Finally I had thought of a way to help myself instead of waiting for someone else to help me. I didn't know if it would work, but I had to try.

"Are you sure you don't want us to go with you?" asked Ti An.

"This is something I've got to do alone," I said.

"Good luck," said Darlene.

"Thanks," I said.

16

Corny Things
Can Be True

I wasn't even sure that the gym was open, and I didn't know what I was going to say, but I knew I had to go there. The sun had gone behind some clouds. Snow had started to fall, icy particles that stung my face.

The Evergreen Gymnastics Academy sign was creaking in the wind. The only windows in the gym are high up, near the roofline, and I couldn't see whether there were any lights on.

I opened the door. I could hear shrieks and giggles coming from the gym.

I stomped the snow off my boots and walked in. Patrick was working with a group of the tiny tots. He had them lined up on the beam, looking like fat little sparrows. Little kids have such funny bodies. They all had bellies that stuck out. They looked so cute.

The ones that weren't on the beam were running around in circles and shrieking at the tops of their lungs.

"Cindi!" Patrick exclaimed.

"Hi, Patrick," I said. "Can I talk to you?"

"I've got my hands full," he said. "This session will be over in ten minutes. Can you wait?"

"Sure," I said.

In the far corner of the gym, Heidi was working out with Dimitri, practicing her vault.

Heidi was listening intently as Dimitri gestured with his hands. It was Heidi who saw me first, and she waved to me.

I went over to her to say hello.

"Cindi!" exclaimed Dimitri. He gave me a bear hug. "It's good to look at you."

"It's a madhouse here," said Heidi. "I can't hear myself think, now that Patrick's got those little monsters running around the gym. The Pinecones aren't here today. I don't know where they are."

"I saw them," I said. I was relieved. At least the Pinecones hadn't told Heidi what they were doing.

One of the little kids dashed by me, and tripped on one of the mats, and almost fell into Heidi.

"Careful," I warned. "You almost crashed into a potential Olympic champion."

The little girl looked up at Heidi. "You're not so big," she said. "I want to play on the horse."

Heidi rolled her eyes.

"It is *not* a toy," growled Dimitri. I had a feeling that working with little kids was not Dimitri's strong suit.

I took the little kid by the hand and led her back to Patrick.

"Here's a stray," I said.

"I got to go to the bathroom," said the little girl.

"So do I," said a little redhead.

"Me, too," said another.

"I'll take them," I said to Patrick.

Patrick looked grateful. My three little ones started to run in all directions. I put my fingers in my mouth and blew an ear-piercing whistle, something Jared had taught me.

The kids stopped in their tracks. "Hold it," I said. "We're gymnasts. We *march* to the bathroom."

The little kids started to march in place.

"Thanks," said Patrick.

I marched the little kids to the bathroom. By the time they had all finished, the parents had started to come out into the gym to collect them.

Patrick looked at me gratefully again as I delivered my three to their parents.

"Cindi, it's good to see you. I've missed you." He got a towel and wiped his face.

I looked around the gym. Patrick had put up a Christmas tree, but it wasn't decorated yet.

"I've missed you, too," I said. "I've been saying those words a lot lately."

"The Pinecones haven't been the same without you," said Patrick.

"Did you know what they were doing over at the mall?" I asked him.

"The pinecone ornaments?" asked Patrick.

"It was a horrible idea," I said. "I was so embarrassed."

"They wanted to do something," he said. "You can't blame them."

"I know," I said. "Patrick, is there something I could do at the gym to help pay for my lessons?"

Patrick looked a little embarrassed. I knew it was probably hopeless, but I had to try. I didn't give him a chance to answer. "I could sweep the floor after school or wash out the locker room. The Pinecones said that I haven't done anything except mope around, and they're right — except making a basket with a hole in the bottom, but . . . I'd do *anything*."

"Cindi," said Patrick, "I don't think you're old enough to be hired as a janitor."

"I hate being eleven!" I exploded. "There's nothing I can do . . . except take little kids to the bathroom."

Patrick sat down on the bench. "You know," he said slowly, "that's one thing that I can't do. Along with helping the little girls in the locker room. I sure could use help with these tiny tots, and the little kids seem to like you."

 "I really like them," I said excitedly. "I'm good with little kids, honest. I baby-sit. I could get references."

"I don't need references, Cindi," said Patrick. "The job wouldn't be easy. You'd have to work every Saturday, and then on weekdays I'd need you a half hour before the Pinecones practice."

"I could do it," I said. "And then I could stay and take lessons again." I was so excited. I couldn't believe it might all work out!

"How much can you pay me?" I asked Patrick. I suddenly got a sinking feeling. I knew how much I made baby-sitting, and I knew how much my lessons at the gym cost.

"I can't afford to pay you what your lessons would cost," said Patrick.

I tried not to look disappointed. I should have known I'd never be able to earn enough.

"Cindi," said Patrick, "I'm glad you came to talk to me. I was going to call you this week anyhow, but it's so much better that you came to me."

"Why?" I asked. "So you could tell me that I can't earn enough to come back?"

"Cindi," he said, "it's not like you to be bitter."

"I'm sorry," I said, "but it's so hard to be cheerful when it's always bad news."

"This isn't bad news," said Patrick. "Big Beef had always said if things were tough I should come to him. I called him, and he told me confidentially that he had already talked to you and your parents, but I said that I finally thought there was something he could do. From time to time, we lose kids who are really important to this place, and I asked him if he could help with that."

I was shaking my head.

"Hear me out," said Patrick.

"But I already turned down Big Beef," I said.

"Big Beef wants to set up the Big Beef Gymnastics Scholarship for our gym, and you have the honor of being selected as the first winner," said Patrick.

"There are plenty of kids in worse shape than me. Dad lost his job, but there are loads of kids in Denver poorer than we are. I don't deserve it."

"That's not true. And the scholarship isn't based just on need, it's also based on merit.

Cindi, you add so much to this team. The Pine-cones don't work as well without you. You're always ready to try anything new, and you're the spark to encourage everybody else to try it. We need you here. Big Beef's scholarship is to help pay for any good gymnasts who can't afford lessons. You'll be our first. And helping with the Tiny Tot Gymnastics would help offset the costs."

I kept shaking my head. "My dad's a proud man," I said. "I don't think he'd want anybody else to pay for my lessons."

"You'd also be working for me," said Patrick. "helping me with the Tiny Tots program."

"I know," I said, "but I'm not sure Dad would take it that way, and I don't want to make him feel bad."

"I don't think your father would want pride to stand in your way," said Patrick. "The truth is that life isn't fair. It isn't fair that your father lost his job. But you can't always refuse help from people who care about you. This isn't charity. It's a scholarship. You're getting it on merit. You're a darned fine gymnast, one of the best on your team. When you don't need it anymore, some other girl or boy will get a chance at gymnastics. None of this would have happened if you hadn't had to quit gymnastics when your dad lost his job. It made Big Beef and I think about what we could do. So sometimes something good comes out of something bad."

"That's so corny," I said.

"Sometimes corny things are true, but it's got to be your decision," said Patrick.

I heard a honk outside. "Those're my brothers," I said.

"Promise me you'll talk this over with your parents," said Patrick.

"I promise," I said.

"And Cindi," he said, "don't take too long. I really do need help with those little kids. They're driving me crazy."

17

Things Will
Get Better

When I got out into the parking lot, all the Pinecones had piled into the backseat of our car.

"They insisted on coming," said Tim.

"What happened?" asked Lauren.

"Did you talk to Patrick?" asked Jodi.

I looked at Darlene. "You didn't tell me your dad was setting up a scholarship program," I said.

"I wanted Patrick to tell you this time," said Darlene. "It's official. Not charity!"

"What's she talking about?" asked Lauren.

"Didn't you tell them?" I asked Darlene.

Darlene shook her head. "Dad told me not to talk about it. He didn't want you to be embarrassed."

"Well, this time it was me who blabbed about it," I admitted. I shrugged. "I don't think it's good to have secrets among the Pinecones."

"So that means you're coming back!" shouted Ti An. "You're a Pinecone again."

"Not necessarily," I said. "I've got to talk to my folks about it. And I'm not sure how I feel about taking a scholarship."

"*Now* what's your problem?" exclaimed Lauren.

"I don't know," I admitted.

Tim dropped off the Pinecones back at the entrance to the mall. "I don't get why you're not happy," said Jared.

"I've got to talk to Mom and Dad," I said.

When we got home, I went into the kitchen. Mom and Dad were sitting at the table with a bunch of papers spread out in front of them. I could see that some of them were bills.

I told them about Patrick's and Big Beef's offer. "It's still charity," I said as I finished. "Even though I'll be working for part of it."

"What's wrong with charity?" asked Dad.

I gave him a puzzled look. "I didn't want to hurt your pride," I said.

"Don't you think I am proud of you?" said Dad. "You're the one who went to Patrick and asked him for a job, and he's paying you for something you're good at. And he said the scholarship is on merit."

"Dad," I said, "you know the job only pays for a little bit of the cost."

Dad took a sip from the coffee cup with his name on it that we had bought at Disney World. I looked at the pink flamingos. It seemed like such a long time ago when we had taken trips together and never worried so much about money.

"Mom?" I asked. "What do you think I should do?"

"We've tried to teach all you kids that giving to others is important," said Mom.

"I know that," I said. "I loved Lauren's idea to turn the Holiday Show into a fund-raiser to save the evergreens — well, actually it was kind of Becky's idea."

"I don't think evergreen trees are more important than you are," said Mom.

"Steve's got a football scholarship at the University of Colorado. Because of it, he can stay in school. Should he refuse it?" asked Dad.

"No, of course not," I admitted.

"You love gymnastics, and you're good at it," said Mom. "I think you deserve this scholarship as much as anybody else does."

"And I don't think that you should let pride

stand in your way. There's a difference between pride and foolish pride," said Dad.

"It's kind of hard to tell the difference, though, isn't it?" I asked Dad.

Dad nodded.

I looked at him. "It would have been easier if we hadn't needed it, wouldn't it?" I asked him.

"Of course," Dad admitted. "Nothing about hard times is easy. That's why they're called hard."

"Things will get better, Dad, I know it," I said, giving him a hug.

Dad hugged me back. "They already are," he said.

18

Soaring

I couldn't believe how out of shape I'd become in the little while I had been gone — even with the exercises I had been doing at home.

My legs were still strong, but my arms were much weaker. My biceps and triceps ached, but I was as ready as I'd ever be.

We were in the locker room, changing for the Holiday Show.

My parents, Tim, Stephen, and Jared were all out in the audience. The little kids were on first. I had helped Patrick get them ready by teaching them how to do somersaults, one after another. I could hear the audience applauding.

Little kids have it easy. All they have to do is

show up and everybody applauds because they look so cute.

Just then Becky came storming into the locker room.

"I don't believe it," she said.

"Now what's wrong?" I asked her. "We've got a great audience. We're raising a lot of money for the Save the Evergreens Fund. Big Beef got the Denver Broncos to donate a pair of tickets. Barking Barney donated a 'pet of your choice' to be auctioned off. My mom has offered to cook chili for twenty-five. The auction's going to be terrific."

"Oh, forget about all that," said Becky. "It's the gym's Christmas tree. It looks so tacky. I've got a lot of friends out there, and they're all laughing at it."

"Why?" asked Lauren. "I think the Christmas tree looks beautiful."

"It's got all these silly pinecone ornaments on it," said Becky, "made out of pipe cleaners. I mean, really. It's so childish."

"I think it's beautiful," I said, winking at Lauren.

We heard the whistle blow. "Come on, Pinecones," shouted Darlene. "We're on next."

We went out into the gym. Patrick was acting as the announcer and ringmaster.

"And now," he said, "the Pinecones."

I heard my brothers yell.

"First up," said Patrick. "Cindi Jockett will demonstrate a layout on the trampoline." He paused.

Patrick came over to the trampoline. I had been practicing all week, but I still felt rusty.

Patrick helped me hook up the harness. He tested the pulley.

"Remember," whispered Heidi who was standing next to the trampoline. "Go for the height!"

I nodded. I *was* nervous. It wasn't for a meet but, still, everybody was watching me. So many people in the gym knew that my dad had lost his job. I didn't want anybody's pity. I wanted everybody to know that the Jocketts could still fly.

I climbed up onto the trampoline and started jumping, going higher and higher. I was way above the top of the Christmas tree in the corner. I could make out the pinecone ornaments. A gift *of* pinecones *from* the Pinecones.

I could hear people in the audience gasp as I flew higher and higher into the air, each time plummeting in a free-fall to the net of the trampoline, and then sailing upwards toward the roof, soaring and dropping, soaring and dropping. Then finally, when I knew I could go no higher, I twisted my body around itself, twirling in the air, keeping my body stiff as a board.

I dropped back down to the trampoline, earthbound again.

I was breathing so hard, I could hardly hear the applause. I searched through the faces in the audience and saw my dad, standing up and clapping. He looked so proud. My performance was a gift to him.

After the show, we all gathered around the Christmas tree.

"I still think those ornaments are tacky," muttered Becky.

Jodi started to sing, "I'm dreaming of a Pinecone Christmas."

The other Pinecones chimed in. I joined them.

Becky put her hands over her ears.

"That's a nightmare," she said.

"Not to me," I said. "To me, it's a dream come true."

About the Author

Elizabeth Levy decided that the only way she could write about gymnastics was to try it herself. Besides taking classes she is involved with a group of young gymnasts near her home in New York City, and enjoys following their progress.

Elizabeth Levy's other Apple Paperbacks are *A Different Twist, The Computer That Said Steal Me*, and all the other books in THE GYMNASTS series.

She likes visiting schools to give talks and meet her readers. Kids love her presentation. Why? "I do a cartwheel!" says Levy. "At least I try to."

APPLE PAPERBACKS

THE GYMNASTS™

by Elizabeth Levy

Available wherever you buy books, or use this order form.

THE BABY-SITTERS CLUB®

by Ann M. Martin

Collect Them All!

The seven girls at Stoneybrook Middle School get into all kinds of adventures...with school, boys, and, of course, baby-sitting!